# PRAISE FOR CO|

*LIBERATION:* nominate
*ELFLING:* 1ˢᵗ prize, Teen Fiction, *CPA Book Awards 2019*
*I AM MARGARET* & *BANE'S EYES:* finalists, *CALA Award 2016/2018*
*LIBERATION* & *THE SIEGE OF REGINALD HILL:* 3ʳᵈ place, *CPA Book Awards 2016/2019*

## PRAISE FOR *I AM MARGARET*

*Great style—very good characters and pace.*
*Definitely a book worth reading, like* The Hunger Games.
EOIN COLFER, author of the *Artemis Fowl* books

## PRAISE FOR *THREE LAST THINGS*

*Beautiful! Corinna Turner is one dang good writer!*
REGINA DOMAN, author of The Angel in the Waters & the award-winning Fairytale Novels series.

*Fantastically good! It made me cry real tears, circumventing all my defenses. I have never read a more psychologically-compelling account of conversion anywhere. It makes very complex and sophisticated truths about grace, sin, freedom, mercy, justice, atonement, redemption, repentance, and salvation crystal clear and compelling, without being cloying or "nice," or contrived.*
DR. VICTORIA SEED, Theologian & Speaker

*The author has a rare gift of nailing human nature perfectly, and I was soooo on the edge of my seat with this one! It had me alternating between laughing out loud and cringing and cheering and wanting to cry. I was totally drawn in from page one and loved it all the way.*
SUSAN PEEK, author of the God's Forgotten Friends series

*WOW, fantastic! Once I started reading, I couldn't stop.*
ANDREA JO RODGERS, author of *At Heaven's Edge* & *On Heaven's Doorstep*

*One of the most moving stories I've ever read.*
PENNY CAIRD

# ALSO BY CORINNA TURNER:

**I AM MARGARET series**
*For older teens and up*

Brothers *(A Prequel Novella)\**
1: I Am Margaret*
*Io Sono Margaret (Italian)*
2: The Three Most Wanted*
3: Liberation*
4: Bane's Eyes*
5: Margo's Diary*
6: The Siege of Reginald Hill*
7: A Saint in the Family†
'The Underappreciated Virtues of
Rusty Old Bicycles' *(Prequel short
story) Also found in the anthology:*
Secrets: Visible & Invisible*

Treasures: Visible & Invisible
*(Prequel short story in anthology)*

I Am Margaret: The Play *(Adapted
by Fiorella de Maria)*

**UNSPARKED series**
*For tweens and up*

*Main Series:*
1: DRIVE!*
2: A Truly Raptor-ous Welcome*
3: PANIC!*
4: Farmgirls Die in Cages*
Book 5†

*Prequels:*
BREACH!* *(Crisis pregnancy theme)*
A Mom With Blue Feathers†
A Very Jurassic Christmas
'A Dino Whisperer at the Zoo'
'Liam and the Hunters of Lee'Vi'

Gifts: Visible & Invisible
*(unSPARKed story in anthology)\**

**FRIENDS IN HIGH PLACES series**
*For tweens and up*

The Boy Who Knew (Carlo Acutis)*
*El Chico Que Lo Sabia (Spanish)*
*Il Ragazzo Che Sapeva (Italian)*

**YESTERDAY & TOMORROW
series**
*For adults and mature teens only*
Someday: A Novella*
*Eines Tages (German)*
1: Tomorrow's Dead†

**STANDALONE WORKS**
*For teens and up*
Elfling*
'The Most Expensive Alley Cat in
London' (Elfling *prequel short
story*)

*For tweens and up*
Mandy Lamb & The Full Moon*
The Wolf, The Lamb, and The Air
Balloon (Mandy Lamb *novella*)

*For adults and new adults*
Three Last Things *or* The Hounding
of Carl Jarrold, Soulless Assassin*
A Changing of the Guard
The Raven & The Yew†

*Awarded the Catholic Writers Guild Seal of Approval
†Coming Soon

# THREE LAST THINGS

*or*

## THE HOUNDING OF CARL JARROLD, SOULLESS ASSASSIN

CORINNA TURNER

unSeen

# CONTENTS

*Without Thy grace we waste away,*
*Like flowers that wither and decay.*

*From 'On Jordan's Bank the Baptist's Cry'*
*by C. Coffin, tr. J. Chandler*

"*D*o they enjoy it?"

Fr. Jacob lifts his lined face and looks at me. Part of the reason I like him is that he doesn't insist on talking all the time. Often he just bows his head and prays for me. But I'm feeling unusually chatty today. Perhaps it's knowing this is almost the last time I'll see him.

"Who?" he asks.

"The victim witnesses."

"Ah." He purses his lips. "Some will tell you that they expect to. Most just talk about closure. That word comes up a lot. Unfortunately, I fail to see how watching a healthy human being with many decades of life ahead of them walk into a room under their own steam, only to be turned before their eyes into a lump of dead meat that needs wheeling out, can ever bring real healing to anyone."

Unbidden, a smile tugs at the corners of my mouth. "Don't you think it's rather insensitive of you to speak like that to me?"

Fr. Jacob shakes his head, blue eyes twinkling back at me, though mostly he looks very serious today. "To you, Carl? Are you bothered?"

1

*I snort slightly and shake my head as well. "No. Not remotely."*

*Fr. Jacob sighs, the twinkle disappearing. He stares at me, and there's something on his face I haven't seen before. Despair?*

*"Cheer up," I tell him. "Plenty more inmates for you to talk into joining your club." That's why he's on edge today. He wants my soul for his God, and he hasn't got it. Baptism, that's what he wants me to want. "You're supposed to be retired, anyway."*

*He was already only a part-time chaplain when I arrived three years ago, and I'm the only one he's still visiting. This last year he's been getting frailer and frailer, and I'm pretty sure he's sick, really sick, but if I ask how he is, he just smiles, says, "As well as anyone almost four score can expect to be," and changes the subject. Clearly the two of us are in a race as to who can meet our maker first. I'm fifty years younger, but it looks like I'm going to win, after all.*

*"Other people have time," he's saying softly. "You haven't, and if anyone ever needed more time, it's you. I sometimes think that's what I hate most about this punishment. It takes away time and with it all hope of repentance."*

*I don't want to start all this again. Not today. "Repentance is for people who've done something wrong," I say harshly. "If there is a God—and you've far from convinced me—he'll see things my way."*

*"And if He doesn't?"*

*"I'm confident he will."*

*Fr. Jacob gives a really deep sigh this time. "Carl..." he sounds anguished. "Murder is a really grave sin. And you have committed it many times over. How can I make you understand before it is too late?"*

*"You can't, so stop wasting your breath. You're starting to sound like Pastor Garrett. You know Pastor Garrett?"*

*Fr. Jacob gives a crooked smile. "Yes, I know him."*

2

"Well, he shows up once a month and shouts at me for an hour. Rants, waves his arms, strides up and down. Tells me I'm going to hell fifteen times for every one time he tells me God loves me. I've been counting. Not much else to do when he gets going. So don't you start telling me I'm evil filth too."

"Evil? No. I think of you more as a wounded child, alone and helpless in a dark wood. But don't think that lets you off the hook. God provided everything necessary for you to find your way out, and you ignored it all. So I am very afraid for you, my friend."

For the first time unease twists in my stomach. "Afraid for me?"

"Afraid for your soul."

I stare at him. He's never ranted at me. Never raved. Never preached hellfire and damnation. He's spoken about God's love and—when he understood that I don't believe love exists—he discussed rational proofs of God. It's all been quite interesting, intellectually speaking. Okay, he's told me how grave my sins are many times, but…with all his poor deluded talk of love, I've always assumed…

"Father…" There's an odd cold prickle down my spine. "Do you… Do you think I'm going to hell?"

He looks back at me, an odd expression on his face. "I cannot know where you are bound. I do not know what is in your heart, in your conscience, what is between you and God."

"I didn't ask you to say if I am; I asked you what you thought."

He's silent for a long, long while, this time. Finally I read the expression on his face: mingled horror and dismay. He must've thought I knew the answer to this question already. I keep silent, waiting.

"Well, if you do want my opinion," he says, when it's quite clear I really do, "You have murdered at least twelve people, in cold blood, for money. You have shown not the slightest remorse. The fact that you

3

*consider your own life just as unimportant as those of your victims shows consistency, but cannot excuse you. So yes, I very much fear you are going to hell, Carl Jarrold."*

I blink in the evening light and lift my head. I've come close to dozing as I run over the memory of my last, disturbing, conversation with Fr. Jacob. The setting sun pours into the small cell they brought me to yesterday evening, after Fr. Jacob had gone. At least two guards are watching me at all times over the cameras. I suppose they expect me to rush to the window to watch the sunset, while thinking melancholy thoughts about it being the last one I'll ever see.

I almost snort out loud, at that. Why does everyone, from Fr. Jacob to the prison guards, find it so hard to believe that I really don't care? Why would I?

Love is the biggest lie out there. If people could see that, perhaps they'd understand. Human beings use one another and often when someone is useful to them they dress it up as "love." Fr. Jacob thinks he "loves" me, the poor lost sheep, but all he wants is another name to his account—though he doesn't realize it, poor deluded man. Everyone I've ever met has used me, from my mother onwards. Love doesn't exist. And Fr. Jacob is right about one thing. Without it, life is utterly meaningless. Why, then, should I care about losing life? Why should anyone? So how can killing someone be wrong?

That draws my thoughts back several weeks.

4

*"Killing is wrong, Carl." Fr. Jacob sounded tired. Then again, he's always tired, now. "Can't you see that everyone but you believes that?"*

*"No, they don't. The State certainly doesn't or they wouldn't be going to do it to me. They can't have it both ways. It either is or it isn't. And clearly they believe it's fine, so long as it suits them. Typical human motivation, can't you see?"*

*Fr. Jacob rubs his forehead. "It is wrong to kill except in case of necessity. The fact that the State doesn't recognize that doesn't make it incorrect."*

*I shake my head at him pityingly. If I'd ever needed any confirmation of my beliefs, my death sentence has given it. Killing is no big deal, so long as it benefits the people doing it. So what did I do wrong? Nothing.*

I open my eyes to the condemned man's cell again. I didn't have much in my own cell, but this place makes it look downright luxurious. Who cares? I like to be by myself. I like to be left to sit quietly and think. Death Row's been great for that. The less I have to do with people the better. Why are they even called people? Users. They're just users. Even Fr. Jacob, though I liked his visits. He's so oblivious to his deeper motivations. Actually believes what he's saying. It's charming, really. In a sad sort of way.

After he dropped his bombshell yesterday, an awkward silence fell. But soon Fr. Jacob turned to more practical matters.

"I've made arrangements for…for a proper burial."

"Really?" I'm surprised—but far from displeased. Since I've got no relatives, I was expecting to get cooked to ashes and stuck in the prison cemetery, but I've always preferred the idea of burial: natural recycling, after all. "But, uh, who's paying for it?" The State took all my money, not that Fr. Jacob would touch any of that wearing a full hazmat suit, double-gloved, and using tongs.

Fr. Jacob just smiles. "I've managed to acquire a plot in a local burial ground. Up by a wall."

"You make it sound so difficult. If it was too expensive, then forget it, seriously."

He smiles again. "No, not the money. I'm perfectly happy to part with that. But…well, it was rather hard to talk them into selling it to me. They were afraid they'd never be able to sell the adjacent one."

"Why not?" I ask blankly.

He just looks at me.

"Ah…" Yes, I'm one of the most reviled men in the country. I'm always forgetting that, since I don't feel I've done anything to deserve it. "How did you persuade them?"

Fr. Jacob laughs. "By buying the adjacent plot as well! That dealt with their objection, so they had to sell to me then."

"You bought two?" Discomfort stirs in my belly. That's a lot of money for a poor priest to spend, and I've still no intention of giving him what he wants. Baptism is about getting forgiveness for sins. I haven't done anything wrong, so I'm not doing it, even if it would make Fr. Jacob happy. "But what are you going to do with the second one?" It'll be a terrible waste, if it just lies there, empty and unused.

"Well, I can think of a perfectly appropriate use for it. It was time I made arrangements anyway."

6

*I eye his pale skin—almost grayish today—and dark shadowed eyes. Just how sick is he? "You plan to be buried there?"*

*"Yes, Carl, I do. I'm sure you'll be relieved to hear it. I know how you feel about waste."*

*I stare at him. Before he told me I was going to hell, I wouldn't have been so surprised. Though I would also have been…surprisingly pleased. But now… "You're really happy to be buried near me? Even though I'm going to hell?"*

*A flicker of pain creases Fr. Jacob's brow. "What I said…don't think I've given up on you, Carl."*

*"But if I don't get baptized?" I challenge him. "Because I'm not going to!"*

*"Damnation isn't contagious, you know," he says gently. "Especially once one is dead. But if you don't accept baptism…it doesn't change the fact that I care about you. That I consider you to be a friend. That I will not reject you as the rest of humanity has done. Even after death. Ultimately, only God will know your fate for certain."*

*I look down at the floor, my throat oddly tight. "Well, in that case," I manage, "thanks."*

The whole cell is orange now from the setting sun, but I stay put. I registered Fr. Jacob as my spiritual advisor seven days ago, so actually he could have been sitting here with me, for the whole of today. I didn't mind his daily visits this week, but after that last one yesterday…the thought of spending a whole day with him telling me I was going to hell, just the way Pastor Garrett does.

Well, I don't think he would have done, but every time he looked at me, I'd know what he was thinking. So I asked him not to come today. I felt bad, after him saying what he said about the burial, but considering what he'd told me earlier...what choice did I have?

*"Are you sure?" The poor man sounded like he was in agony. "Are you sure you don't want me to be here? I could just come to be in the witness gallery, later? Pop in to see you beforehand? In case you...change your mind?"*

*Up until ten minutes ago, I might have said yes. But now I return a firm, "No. I will not change my mind, and you will not enjoy watching me die, so why should you go through that?"*

*"Carl..."*

*"I don't want you here. Don't come."*

*He looks at me for a while, in that sad way. "All right," he says at last. "It's your decision."*

*But as he's leaving he looks me straight in the eye and says, "Please, Carl, don't leave it too late." He closes his eyes and whispers,* "Lord...please don't let him leave it too late."

*His tone...utmost appeal...it makes my spine shudder. But he's spearing me with those blue eyes one last time, speaking with peculiar authority. "Don't leave it too late, Carl."*

*He clasps my hands, blesses me and leaves. And that's that.*

I try to put Fr. Jacob's paranoia from my mind. A meal arrives. In some places the so-called last meal is given as much as twenty-four hours before. Here, the last meal is exactly what it claims to be. I stare at the covered tray in exasperation. I told them I didn't want anything. I mean, what a waste. Actually, the guard persisted so long, I said,

"Fine, you choose." Hoping he'd get the message at last. But apparently he just chose.

Now it's here it seems even more of a waste not to eat it. I lift the cover and find…oatmeal. With a drizzle of syrup on top. Huh. So what does that mean? Oatmeal because the guard assumes when I was a kid, it was the epitome of yuck, and he's getting a kick out of trying to make me suffer? Or oatmeal because it's something warm and comforting to eat on a cold winter morning and the guard figured this evening was a sort of cold winter morning?

Must be the first, what would the guard gain from the second? Joke's on him, though: only mothers who care make their kids a hot breakfast. I never had the chance to hate it growing up. It's mere disinterest, not revulsion, that I feel as I pick up the spoon and begin to eat.

It's not like I expect. It seems very dry. I have trouble swallowing it. I smear a bit across the side of the bowl with the spoon; it seems moist enough.

Doors clang somewhere in the block. I check my watch. Two hours until six o'clock. I've been kind of looking forward to this moment for my whole life. The moment this joke that is life will be over and done with. I couldn't be bothered with much in the way of appeals. I mean, what's the point? Roll on, six o'clock.

The oatmeal gets drier and drier, though. As if it's drying out faster than I can eat it, though its appearance remains unchanged. I almost can't get it all down. It's weird. Is it me? My body? Some stupid protest against its end?

9

Ridiculous. I settle myself on the bed again, my shoulders to the wall, lean my head back and seek something interesting to think about. Usually I do some exercise each day, push-ups and jogging on the spot and stuff, just to keep me from turning into a lump of lard like so many of the guys in here. Today, I can't be bothered—odd, that. But my thoughts are restless. I almost wish Fr. Jacob was here. We've had some interesting discussions over the last three years. When he's not just sitting quietly, praying for me to see the light.

*"Why, Carl?" he asked, soon after he started visiting me. Soon after I started speaking to him, anyway. "Why did you choose this? You're a smart guy, you even made it to college in the face of huge obstacles, you've a degree in Natural Resource Management, you could have done so much good in the world. Why did you choose to kill?"*

*"Money," I tell him simply. "It's supposed to fix everything, isn't it? Make life perfect?"*

*"Oh, yes? And how did that work out for you?"*

*"It didn't. Work. At all. Not that I was surprised, seeing everyone believes in love too."*

*"So why did you carry on?"*

*I shrug. "Why not? It was always possible that little bit more money, that next little bit, might be the charm. I was pretty sure it was nonsense, though. But why be alive and poor when you can be alive and rich?"*

*"Well, maybe because you're going to be poor and dead, now."*

*I shrug again. "Fine by me. I'm pretty sure it's the* alive *bit that's the real problem."*

*Fr. Jacob looks at me so sadly. It irritates me.*

*"I'm amused you think college was such a good thing for me," I tell him. "First job I ever did was because of it.* That *kind of job. I'd worked and saved and scrimped and still it wasn't enough. I needed cash or it'd all have been for nothing. I'd've had to drop out. So I took a job from a local gang leader to off his rival. They were both as bad as one another; felt like I was doing a public service, really. Anyway, he paid me to do it, then when I'd got him cornered, the other guy gave me a load of money to kill the first guy, so after I killed him, I went back and killed the first guy too. So I got paid twice. Just like in* The Good, The Bad and the Ugly.

*"And I was clever about it. Got myself a silencer, used my head. No one figured out it was me, the innocent, wet-behind-the-ears college student. Cops didn't even charge me with those two, so I guess they never cottoned on either. Bet I wouldn't be here now on account of the rest, if someone hadn't turned me in.*

*"Anyway, it paid for the rest of college, and I didn't plan to do it again. Meant it to be a one-off. But it was just too easy. Simply do a little thinking, make a plan and pull a trigger."*

*Fr. Jacob's face had gone very still. "Most people don't find that easy."*

*I shrug. "Well, I do. What's the big deal? Death? It's gotta be a distinct improvement."*

*If anything, Fr. Jacob's now looking at me even more sadly than before.*

I thought then that he just wanted me to love life, the way everyone else seems to. But now…he was worrying about my soul, wasn't he?

But why would God send me to hell for acting as all humans do? For seeking my own advantage. Life is worthless. Taking something of no value away from someone isn't wrong. *I* did nothing wrong. The state is doing nothing wrong. We're all just humans, using each other.

Why on earth am I thinking about this again? Okay, it shocked me when Fr. Jacob said he thought I was going to hell. The way he's always been with me. All his talk of love. Calling me friend. I didn't think he thought that. I suppose I didn't see it coming. But what does it matter? He's wrong. For me, there's heaven or there's nothing. Because I'm not convinced God's there at all. Fr. Jacob had some very rational arguments for God, but at the end of the day, God and love are so wound up together. How do you really have all this God-stuff without love? So since love doesn't exist, where does that leave God?

And if there's no God, where does that leave me?

Nowhere.

I suppose if I'm honest, I'd *rather* there was God—and heaven. Something better than this. Peace and happiness. The things I've always craved. But I doubt there *is*. How can there be? What does it matter, anyway? What does anything matter?

"Do you have any regrets, Carl?" Fr. Jacob asked me earlier in the week. "Anything you wish you'd done or hadn't done?"

I wasn't in a chatty mood that day, and I didn't answer the question. I tried to ignore it. But it creeps back, now. No, I've no regrets, exactly. But…two wishes. If I'm honest with

12

myself. And I'm having trouble not being honest with myself, today.

I wish I understood why everyone thinks life is so great. And I wish I knew what it felt like to believe that biggest lie of all. To feel loved.

They're not very rational wishes, are they? I guess they've been there in me, all the time, but they only lately popped to the surface.

No matter. I take another drink of water. I've been feeling thirsty all afternoon, and the oatmeal seems to have dried out my mouth even more. I check my watch again, but it's still only four-thirty. Maybe I should have let Fr. Jacob come. No need for him to have watched. I'm tempted to pick up that phone and call him. Unlimited telephone usage, they told me, but who would I call? Well, I could call Fr. Jacob…no. He's the reason my thoughts are so unsettled. Speaking to him will just make it worse.

An hour and half to kill. Time's another thing I've never had trouble killing. I try to focus on a fact, a film, a book, something of interest, but everything just seems to spiral back around to God and heaven and hell and life and love and Fr. Jacob saying, "Don't leave it too late, Carl."

At five-thirty I put on the hospital gown and slippers provided—if I don't, no doubt they'll come to hustle me into it—then I relieve myself as thoroughly as I can, since I figure it will save mess later—not that it'll be my problem by then. But immediately I'm sipping water again. The dry mouth is really getting annoying. Maybe I'm coming down with something. What a shame. I laugh out loud, but it sounds strange to my ears.

Feeling naked and uncomfortable in the skimpy gown, I sit back on the bed. I joshed Fr. Jacob so much, when he first started visiting, because of the long black cassock he always wears. He absorbed everything I dished out with a soft smile and a steely gaze, until eventually I figured out that this white-haired old priest was way tougher than me, long black dress or no long black dress.

I should have called him. We parted awkwardly, yesterday...

Doors clang. Someone's coming. I expect to feel relief, but instead I'm suddenly very aware of my heart, thudding in my chest. Thudding faster than usual. Coldness spreads up my limbs, but perspiration breaks out on my forehead. What's the matter with me?

Two prison guards enter. I mentally dub the Latino guy Oatmeal—since he's the one responsible—the second I've long thought of as Ostrich—since he looks like the latter. Well, if ostriches got sunburned. They're both armed with the new Bio-Locked Smart handguns they brought in after that nasty incident in a prison up north. So even if I felt like shooting them and actually managed to get hold of one of their guns, it wouldn't even fire for me.

Once they've cuffed me: "Come with us, please," says Oatmeal, quiet but firm, with just that hint of a Spanish lilt.

I go with them. My legs feel strange, but I make myself walk steadily. It's not far. Just next door. It's like some incredibly bleak, bare hospital room. Pretty much nothing in here but a sinister gurney with lots of restraining straps. Two huge windows face each other. One covered by a blind, the other by one-way glass.

Studying the room, I note two small holes under the one-way window, with a bit of medical tubing protruding from each. That's where they'll pull out the IV lines. I've read about the "procedure." According to the state, it's painless, apart from the pricks as they insert the IV needles. According to opponents, there's a strong chance many of the convicted suffer quite severely. After what I've read, I'd certainly have picked a firing squad over this, if I'd had a choice.

But I didn't, so I'm about to find out who's right. It won't be much help, because I won't be able to tell anyone, but there we are.

"Lie down on the bed," says Ostrich, un-cuffing me again. "Head that end, feet that end."

I stare at that gurney. I lie down on there and regardless of who's right, it will all be over in about half an hour, tops. But I don't want to. I'm shocked by *how much* I don't want to.

"On the bed," says Ostrich, more menacingly, and they take hold of the patient gown I'm wearing and walk me right up to it.

I've seen films where lone super assassins or government agents would get themselves out of this situation without breaking a sweat. But I'm good with a gun, not with fancy moves, and they can whistle up ten more guards in a heartbeat. I'm going to end up on that gurney, no matter what.

I get onto it; lie down. My breathing's gone tight and quick. All these years thinking this would be a good thing, and I don't want to be here at all. I would rather be anywhere but here. Why did I tell Fr. Jacob not to come? I want to see his friendly face right now. Though what words of comfort could he give me, after what he said yesterday?

Tan hands and sunburned hands move in and out of my vision as Oatmeal and Ostrich fasten the straps around my legs and waist. They stretch out my arms along the crosspieces and fasten more straps, leaving me utterly helpless. My thoughts whirl faster and faster, making it hard to keep up with them. *Why do I feel like this?*

Life is nothing. Life is meaningless. I recite it in my head, seeking calmness, but it doesn't work.

The medical assistant (not that he'll have much actual medical training, according to what I've read) enters the room and opens my gown at the neck, not making eye contact as he takes his time sticking five little round tab things to my chest in a precise pattern, each one like a cold finger pressing on my skin. When he seems satisfied he's got them in the right places, he connects a wire to each one and closes the gown up again as best he can.

So…that's the heart monitor, so they can tell when…when…

He's bending over my left arm, now. He makes a sound of relief. "Good veins on this one," he mutters to Oatmeal and Ostrich. His accent is faintly British—how'd he end up here, doing this? But despite his words, his fingers poke and probe, poke and probe, clumsy compared to any nurse who's ever taken my blood. He jabs the needle in, waggles it, swears, takes it out, adjusts the tourniquet, tries again. My involuntary flinches draw muttered apologies; still no eye contact. He knows how clumsy he is.

I catch Oatmeal and Ostrich exchanging a look across me: *where on earth did they find this idiot?* Or perhaps, since I've heard this sort of thing does happen: *this guy's even more useless than the last one.*

It feels like at least ten minutes before the man rams the fat needle in yet again and is finally satisfied. He tapes the IV in place and attaches the line. That's one in place. One to go. The real one, and the backup. My heart's thundering now, and I'm so cold. A quivering actually runs throughout my foolish body.

The man's doing his inexpert jabbing again, driving the needle into my right arm repeatedly. What on earth does he do to someone with *bad* veins?

"Do I *look* like a pin cushion?" The words snap from me after a particularly fierce poke. Heat rises up the man's face. He mutters something about my veins being deceptive, whatever that means. Ten minutes later he gives up and starts on my wrist instead. Doesn't this count as torture? Ah, what does it matter? It's a few more minutes of life, in exchange for minor pain. Right now, it seems a very good trade.

But, finally, he's taping the second IV in place. Connecting the line. I must've been in here for almost half an hour. I thought the whole business was supposed to be over by now.

But... *He's connected the second line.*

17

They can kill me now, whenever they want. At any moment. It's entirely up to them.

Ah…no. Procedure. They're winding the gurney up into a more upright position. Facing the window covered by the blind. A shocking surge of relief flows through me. I still have a few moments. A few moments while they display me to the witness galleries and ask if I have any last words. I wasn't planning on saying anything. Now all I want to say is "Please don't do this."

*Why* didn't I use all my appeals? I could have delayed this by *years*.

The blind whirs as it rises. Two witness galleries. One is packed with people who stare at me with stony faces. Or open hatred. The relatives of some of my victims. I stare back at them dispassionately. *I did nothing wrong.* Why does a flock of saber-toothed butterflies go mad in my belly at that?

The other gallery is almost empty. Three members of the press and a few official witnesses. Watching with eagerness and dispassion, respectively. No one is there for me. No one in the world gives a rat's tail if I live or die. Except perhaps Fr. Jacob, and I wouldn't let him come.

A detached voice booms from the speakers in the ceiling, reading out my sentence. My remaining moments of life are almost over. The voice asks for my last words. I didn't prepare any. There was nothing I wanted to say, other than "let me out of here," which is still what I want to say, but with the exact opposite meaning. But if I say nothing, it's over. Death will flow through one of those lines and take me.

And I don't want it. I'm beyond confused, beyond understanding it right now, but I know I don't.

"Any last words?" demands the voice again.

I try to unglue my tongue from the roof of my dry mouth, twisting my head, trying to see that one-way window behind me, then notice the video camera in front of me and eyeball that instead.

My voice cracks slightly, then strengthens. "I hear they only pay you three hundred dollars for doing this. Guess the State places even less value on life than I do."

My words are for the executioner, but it's the victim witnesses who react. They scowl; one of them shouts something, but the glass blocks the sound. A woman starts crying, fist to her mouth, staring at me in helpless fury. Oh. I guess they didn't like what I said. Is there anything I can say to them? "You're all over-reacting, I really didn't do anything terrible," probably wouldn't go down very well, either…

Too late; Oatmeal and Ostrich wind the gurney back into a flat position, and my heart takes off again, pounding as though it's trying to get away all on its own, and *I* feel like something terrible is about to happen.

Any moment now. Any moment now…

I close my eyes, struggling to calm my breathing, but I can't stop my thoughts, turning inexorably on. I want to scream. Waiting for that deadly liquid to enter my veins, I actually want to scream out loud.

And understanding comes, in a chilling burst of memory. Of people begging, crying, getting on their knees, offering money, fighting back in ludicrous ways…because they wanted to live. Because they felt exactly as I feel now. I could never understand it. Why they behaved like that. When I was so sure I would not.

They wanted to live. Just as I want to live.

*Why? Why do I want to live?*

The answer dances just out of reach, like a taunting child. Something about life. There must *be* something about life. Something I've never understood. There *has* to be or I couldn't feel this way.

It's anatomically impossible for nerves to tear but mine feel screwed up tight enough to do so as I wait for that cold touch of liquid entering one of my arms. There'll be seven injections, three of drugs, alternated with saline wash. I'm supposed to only feel the first, the drug that should render me unconscious…so the other two drugs can stop my breathing and then…my heart.

My frantic thoughts dissolve into bewildered fear; fear that pierces right through me like a jagged sword driving through my gut, pinioning me to this death bed.

I'm panting, I can't help it, and that trembling grips me. I keep my eyes tight shut, seeking to keep my fear private. A great longing makes itself known through the maelstrom. Fr. Jacob. Why on earth didn't I let him come? I'm a human, a user, so why didn't I ask him to come? For my comfort, who cares about him not enjoying it?

Why didn't I?

Because it would hurt him.

So? What do I gain now by him *not* being hurt? I gain nothing.

The puzzle dissipates as another thought flies through my mind: why are they waiting? Minutes must have passed; I thought the procedure would be immediate? But I'm just lying here.

And lying here.

And lying here…

My fear reaches such an intensity I'd almost welcome that cold touch, anything to put an end to it, yet even now, I'm clinging onto my life as though just holding on tight enough might save me.

"What's going on?" Slight lilt—the mutter comes from Oatmeal.

"Not sure." Ostrich speaks under his breath too. "Maybe the drugs aren't working. I mean, aren't they using veterinary drugs this time, or something?"

I try to hide from the fear in thought. Veterinary drugs. No surprise there. From my reading, the State are having to use all sorts of new drugs to kill people. Other countries— where they don't have capital punishment because they agree with Fr. Jacob and think no one should be killed like this in a stable, civilized nation—are refusing to sell them the human-certified drugs. But nothing's come down those lines yet, so it's not that. I could tell them so, but if I open my mouth I'm not sure what words will come out.

The fear swallows me again. It'll happen soon. Any moment…

Any moment…

Any moment…

"Heck, it's been almost fifteen minutes, what are they doing in there?" whispers Oatmeal.

"Who cares?" mutters Ostrich. "Who cares if this monster sweats a bit?"

"Monster or not, this is torture, plain and simple."

No surprise I'm failing to hide my fear. I can't control my breathing, and cold, clammy sweat covers me. I can't stop that trembling either. All I can do is keep my eyes and mouth clamped shut.

A door opens. Hands touch my arm—I risk a peep. It's fake medical man, his face now concealed with a hygiene mask, because the blind is up. Trapped inside my agony of waiting, I'd almost forgotten about the witnesses. Medical Guy's face looks pale as he jiggles the needles—ouch—and examines the IV apparatus. Clearly something isn't working properly. Are the drugs in one of the lines already?

For a moment I'm afraid I'm going to puke all over Oatmeal, who's stepped close to Medical Guy.

"This is taking too long," he whispers. "What's up?"

"You think we aren't trying to figure that out?" Medical Guy bolts back into the one-way mirror room.

"They'll sort it out." Oatmeal's speaking to me now, his voice clearly meant to be reassuring. "Just hang in there."

"Good grief, you pathetic bleeding heart, Tom—let the creep sweat." Ostrich's tone is scathing.

"Don't you realize it's been *forty-five minutes* since we took him from the cell?" retorts Oatmeal, under his breath.

"Let him lie there and piss himself."

"Godless barbarian!"

"Pathetic *muchacha!*"

They fall silent, no doubt glaring at one another, but I don't dare peep in case I accidentally make eye contact and start begging. I've never thought of myself as brave, because if you're not scared, where does courage come into it? But I never thought I'd be a coward either. Yet this crash-course in fear threatens to overwhelm me. And why did Ostrich have to mention peeing? I'm starting to want to go so bad. That blasted dry mouth earlier.

*Just keep breathing, Carl. Try and breathe more slowly. Savor each breath. Just treat each breath like a precious gift. Like something you didn't ever expect to have. A bonus.*

Only…each breath isn't *like* a precious gift. It *is* a precious gift. My breath speeds up again and my mind spins, as I feel that answer inch closer to my grasp.

*Life is precious.*

But *why?* I don't doubt the conclusion. Right now I can *feel* the truth of it in every quivering vein. But *why?*

Argh, if they don't hurry up, I really am going to piss myself, but I don't want to feel that liquid entering me, I *don't*…but what if when I feel it, I *can't* hold on? I'll go down in history as the guy who pissed himself before he was even dead. No. No more thinking about liquids. Think about life. Precious life, which I still have at this moment. *Enjoy it, Carl.*

But…if life is this precious, what have I been doing for almost three decades? Why have I never understood? Why have I wasted my life?

Why have I stolen other people's?

Oh God.

*Oh, Fr. Jacob, you were right…*

The door clicks, Medical Guy is back. He looks over everything again and hisses to himself anxiously.

"Look, it's been an hour since we brought him in," says Oatmeal. "What's happening, are they going to reschedule?"

Reschedule? What a wonderful thought. But somehow I doubt—

"For *this animal?*" snorts Medical Guy. "No chance. Governor wants it done today. Warden says if I can't find the problem now, we'll get out two completely fresh sets of IVs, lines and everything, hook them up and Bob's your uncle."

"Carl's a stiff, you mean," puts in Ostrich glibly.

"Well, how long is all that going to take?" demands Oatmeal, ignoring his partner's humor. They're all talking loudly, so they must've switched off the mics to the viewing galleries.

"Shouldn't take more than half an hour, all told."

*Half an hour?* My bladder is protesting so loudly it's actually drowning out some of the fear. "In that case," I manage to speak something approaching calmly, "I'm going to have to use the toilet."

"Oh, you have got to be kidding me!" Medical Guy sounds appalled.

"You said you were about to put new IVs in anyway," points out Oatmeal. "So you'll be taking the old ones out."

"Yes…" Medical Guy looks at the one-way mirror. "Sir?"

A voice comes through the speaker. The prison warden, hiding out in there. "Fine, you two take the Condemned to the nearest restroom while we get the lines changed over. We'll let you know as soon as we're ready."

"Yes, sir."

Everything takes on a completely unreal quality as Medical Guy unclips the heart monitor leads, un-tapes the IVs and pulls them out, Oatmeal and Ostrich undo the restraints, and I'm able to sit up and get down off the gurney. They cuff me again, then I'm standing on legs I never thought I'd stand on again. I'm walking, which I never thought I'd do again. Right across the bleak room and through the door and along the corridor…

*Oh God, if only I wasn't going to have to go back the other way again. Oh, if only this was for real, rather than just for a piss. One last piss. Oh God, I've pissed my life away, I've wasted my entire life. That would be bad enough, but the things I've done… I'm* that animal*, the monster, the evil assassin. I thought… I didn't realize…*

We're going into a stairwell, through another door, along a passage. Why aren't we simply going back to the cell? Oh, right, there's another execution scheduled for tomorrow. They brought me here about this time yesterday; no doubt the next walking dead guy's in there already. I fight to keep my mind on this subject, to distract myself from the pounding dread. *Two in a row, bet the press love that.* But distraction is impossible.

*Oh God, I want to talk to Fr. Jacob so badly.*

Here's the toilet. Oatmeal opens the door and takes a quick look around, examines the lock, then comes back out and waves invitingly.

25

But I hesitate. "Is there—" My voice cracks and I have to clear my throat. "Is there…any chance I could make a phone call?"

"No," Oatmeal's headshake is so firm his close-cropped black hair actually swings slightly. "Out of the question."

I expected it, but my heart sinks so badly it positively hurts. I try to keep my voice steady. "Is there…is there any chance at all…I could get a message to someone?" I seriously feel about an inch from breaking down and bawling. I've got this blessed reprieve, these brief few extra moments, and I still can't speak to Fr. Jacob.

"No," says Ostrich harshly. "Should have used your last words for that, shouldn't you? Instead of tormenting your victims' families."

"I didn't m…" *mean to…* But the words die in my throat. I keep my eyes on Oatmeal's brown ones.

"A message to who?" His tone is unencouraging. He's going to say no, too.

"Fr. Jacob."

Oatmeal frowns. "Fr. Jacob…?"

"Fr. Jacob Thompson. He's my spiritual advisor."

Oatmeal nods slowly. He knows Fr. Jacob, does he?

"Could you just send him a text?" A note of pleading enters my voice. I'm about ready to *beg*.

"We don't have phones when we're on duty, moron." Ostrich directs a scornful look my way.

My heart plummets again…of course they don't…but Oatmeal glances at his watch, then takes his radio from his belt. "Do you know his number?"

I nod.

"What do you want the text to say?"

I swallow, my mind racing. I hate giving the message before he's actually committed himself to sending it, but even worse is choosing the words themselves. How to compress the onslaught of understanding that's consumed me for the last hour into a few short words, preferably words that also make up for our tense parting yesterday?

"Well?"

A fog of fear and confusion hangs over my mind, pierced through by that burning need to pee. But the words come. "Please say: *You were right, and I wish I could join your club after all.*"

"Anything else?"

I shake my head. "That's it."

Oatmeal nods acceptance of this, selects a channel and presses the button on his walkie-talkie, raising it to his lips. "Hey, Andy, you still here?"

"Yeah, you just caught me."

"You in the locker room, then?"

"Yep. 'Bout to turn my radio in."

"Think you can send a text for me?"

"Guess so, but what if they reply?"

"Don't think they will, but...well, give them my number."

"Okay, where's it going?"

I tell Oatmeal Fr. Jacob's number and he relays it to Andy in the locker room.

"What do you want to say?"

Oatmeal repeats my message verbatim. "And you'd better put *from*…" He hesitates. Yes, if Andy is anything like Ostrich, he might not send it if he knows it's for me. "Put from C. J. You got that?"

"Yeah, got it. Okay, it's sent. *Hang on one freaking minute…C. J. That better not have been from Carl Jarrold, the* soulless freaking assassin. *Tom?*"

"Thanks, Andy, talk another time." Tom, AKA Oatmeal, puts the radio back at his belt.

*I do have a soul. Fr. Jacob wouldn't be interested in me if I didn't.* But I just mutter, "Thanks."

Ostrich stands, arms folded, glaring at his partner, anger reddening his sunburned skin still further. But he could have sabotaged the sending of the message with a few quick words, so I feel more warmly towards him than I have yet. He points into the toilet and says, "You'd better need it, after all this. Enjoy yourself. We'll be going straight back to the execution chamber as soon as you're done."

The warmth evaporates as quickly as it came. "At least I won't die lying in my own piss!" I get into the room and shut the door quickly, before he can decide not to let me go after all. It's only a normal toilet lock, they could have it open in about ten seconds with a coin, but I flip it into place anyway.

"Ever thought you're in the wrong job, Tom?" I hear Ostrich demand, on the other side of the door.

"Frequently," retorts Tom. "But then I remember if everyone like me quits, those poor suckers will be stuck with guys like you."

A contemptuous snort. "You are such a bleeding heart."

28

"You always say that as though it's a bad thing…"

It sounds like a conversation they've had a hundred times before. I need to go too badly to keep listening and step quickly to the toilet. For a few moments everything, even the fear, fades in the pure, uncomplicated pleasure of letting go and relieving myself. Strange that bodily needs can be so overwhelming, even at a time like this. But all too soon I'm done.

I'm halfway through awkwardly washing my still-cuffed hands before I wonder what the heck I'm doing. Wasting my extra minutes on pointless hygiene. But I finish anyway and wipe my hands on the towel. A soft, clean towel; this must be a staff toilet.

I look up—and there I am in the mirror. My face corpse-white, dried sweat plastering my dark hair to my forehead, my eyes as wide as a rabbit's in the moment before the car hits. Some suave assassin. I look lousy. I look how I feel, then.

But I'm not, now, am I? An assassin. I couldn't pull that trigger again, not…not now that I *understand*.

Too many thoughts crowd in my mind, fighting for precedence.

I got the message to Fr. Jacob. My heart lifts slightly, knowing that.

But I've still done exactly what he warned me about, haven't I? Left it too late. Or have I? I don't know what to do.

Life is precious. And I want more of it. I've never thought that about anything before, not even money, really. But now…even this little room seems beautiful. The gleaming white of the basin… Why did I never notice these things? I want more…

But I don't deserve it.

And I'm not going to get it.

As soon as they've got all the equipment changed, we're going to go right back to that room and it's going to start all over again. I'm not sure which is worse, the thought that it will go wrong again...or that it will go right.

Like the whale swallowing the Old Testament guy that Fr. Jacob told me about when he was explaining how he became a priest over fifty years ago, the fear swoops back up and swallows me in one gulp. I fall to my knees and vomit. I can't stop until every scrap of oatmeal and bile is in the toilet, then I huddle on the floor, a wad of toilet paper pressed to my mouth, and cry. I can't stop it, but at least I manage to keep it fairly quiet.

For all my misery and terror, I feel a strange lack of self-pity. Because everyone is right. I *have* acted like a monster. I've brought this on myself, with my stupidity, my blindness. With my…my grave sins. I want to live more than anything, but I don't deserve to.

Eventually I'm gripped with rage. Rage at myself. To cap everything, I'm wasting my last precious minutes groveling on the floor, sniveling like a child. I've never liked waste, and this is waste of criminal proportions. Grabbing a new handful of toilet paper, I blot my eyes, choking off further tears by sheer will power, then get unsteadily to my feet and move to the window.

There's no lock—definitely a staff toilet—and I unlatch it quietly and swing it open. I'm looking down into an inner courtyard of the prison. The texture and color of the concrete walls in the floodlights draws my appreciative eye. Even the things humans build are beautiful.

And the things God built?

I look up. Twinkling lights cover the night sky above. My mouth opens slightly in awe. I feel one hour old, seeing everything for the first time, and my heart aches with longing. But I've had twenty-eight years, and I've wasted them all. I won't waste these last few minutes.

I scramble onto the toilet and up into the window aperture, seeking the best possible view of that beautiful sky. Reaching up with my hands, I grab the guttering that runs just above the window and stand upright on the ledge, looking out. The wind caresses my face and limbs with an icy touch. It's cold out and I'm only wearing this undignified gown, but what do I care?

I drink in the sky for a while, let it consume me…but the play of light in the courtyard snares my attention eventually. Then I notice an air conditioning unit, sticking out of the wall nearby. That's the place to sit and gaze at the stars. We're three floors up and I'd never dare try the maneuver normally, let alone with cuffed hands, but right now I reach out without thinking about it, steadying myself on the gutter, step out of the flip-floppy slippers and hop across the gap. Although I cut my leg slightly on the edge of the unit, I'm soon sitting comfortably with my back to the wall.

But when I bring my knees up to my chest, I feel the poke of the electrode pads for the heart monitor. Hands shaking, I yank the gown open and scrabble to rip them off, to throw them out into the air. They twinkle in the lights as they disappear into the gloom. Even they are beautiful.

I look down at my bare chest. Why did I do that? Wasteful...they'll just have to put new ones on. Too late.

*Waste...oh, the irony. I've always been so annoyed by the waste of the earth's natural resources, yet I've wasted something far more valuable...my own life...and those of others.*

At least I can pull my knees up now, without feeling them there. Closing the gown again and drawing it down over my legs, I feel slightly warmer and a bit less naked. Blood seeps through the cloth from my gashed leg, joining the smears from my punctured arms, but I simply tilt my head back to admire God's handiwork again.

So...is there a God?

I just told Fr. Jacob I'd have liked to join his club and I do kind of wish I had. So have I decided there is?

A thudding on the toilet door. My insides clench and flash freeze. Are they done already?

"What are you doing in there?" Ostrich's voice. "It's gone awfully quiet."

I don't bother replying.

"Jarrold?" Tom Oatmeal's voice, rather sharp. "Jarrold, you don't have to come out yet, but you've got to answer."

It's rather a long way to shout, so I keep my mouth shut. They don't need me to open that door.

Sure enough, moments later footsteps rush across the room, and Tom's head appears at the window. The horrified expression on his face as he stares down into the courtyard quickly turns to puzzlement. He looks around—then his head jerks right round as he spots me.

"*Freaking...!* Did he jump?" Ostrich arrives beside him, turns to follow his line of sight and does a double-take, knocking the slippers into space as he leans out, lumpy head craning on the end of his long neck. "What the heck are you doing, Jarrold?"

This seems such a stupid question I just tilt my face up and return my attention to the stars. Out of the corner of my eye I see their heads turning as they analyze the situation. No way out over the roof, even assuming I could get onto it with cuffed hands. No way down through the courtyard. The most likely outcome of any attempt to get further than I've already got is that I'll end a red, jammy smear on the tarmac below.

"Well, he's not going anywhere," says Tom. He raises his voice. "You going to give us trouble, Jarrold, or are you going to come back in?"

I stare at the stars. Even *thinking* about going back in... Reluctantly, I say, "Don't ask me to until it's actually time, and I will."

"Fair enough." Their heads disappear back inside, with accompanying "brrr" noises, despite the fact they're wearing heaps more than I am.

I can hear them talking quietly, though.

"Are you sure we should just leave him out there?" That's Ostrich.

"Well, he's not doing any harm. Although…" Tom sounds reflective.

"What?"

"Well, if we said he was trying to escape…it's a cast iron reason to shoot him."

"Shoot him?" Ostrich sounds absolutely astonished. I'm listening rather closely myself. "I thought you were the one wanting to hold his hand and make him feel better! Or do you just want to try out these fancy guns?"

Oatmeal puts on a patient voice. "I don't much fancy walking the guy back in there for them to mess it up again, that's what. What a complete farce. They had their chance. What do you say we put a bullet in his heart? Much more humane. We could hardly miss at this range."

My heart's pounding again as my ears strain. When I lay on that gurney I'd almost have welcomed this suggestion but now…there are so many things I want to think about. And I don't want to lose a moment of this wonderful thing called life.

"Humane? For *him?* Forget that," says Ostrich. "Shoot him if you want, but don't expect me to lie and say he was trying to escape. Even I can see he's just freaking stargazing, the creep."

"You are so heartless."

"Am I? One of the people this guy murdered was a fifteen-year-old girl. Your sister's about that age, isn't she?"

I remember the girl. I never did know why someone wanted her dead so bad. Witness to a gangland murder, perhaps? Or an honor killing—I always wondered about that.

34

I can see her terrified face. She threw a hairbrush at me, just before I shot her in the head. It seemed so pointless; I never could understand why she bothered. Until now. When I understand all too well…and six years too late, for her. And for me.

"He's a cold-hearted, evil monster," says Oatmeal, after a tense silence, "but he's still a human being. And since God is everyone's father, I'm afraid that makes him our brother, like it or not."

"Yeah, yeah, save the Jesus-talk for someone who cares. I don't know what you're worrying about, anyway. If he doesn't want to go back in, he can jump, and there's nothing we can do to stop him. Oh, we are going to be in *so* much trouble if he jumps."

Yeah, the State didn't pay for all that death watch just so I could end in a quick, private splat in the prison yard.

Silence falls. Broken only by one of them flushing the stinking toilet. I stare at the stars, my thoughts churning. Tom is a Christian, clearly, but I'm startled by his suggestion. Unless he gets pleasure from killing people—and he's clearly not like that—then what does his would-be compassionate act gain him?

Fr. Jacob's trickled more into my head than I'd like to admit, though so much of it has never seemed to make sense, and the answer comes. Compassion gets you a reward from God. Actually, from some of the things Fr. Jacob has said, I'm not sure what Tom proposed really would delight God, but there's no doubt he means well.

God rewards compassion. This explains a lot. Every now and then I'll encounter someone doing something that seems to make no sense. Christians and other religious people are the chief offenders. I've always assumed there was some motivation really, that I just couldn't put my finger on. And I suppose I was right. They're simply using God, not each other.

Unless it's not using. Unless it's love. Fr. Jacob was right about everything else. What if he was right about that too?

I feel a renewed longing for the sacrament he kept offering me. The baptism-thing. And a deep regret.

*Don't leave it too late, Carl.*

But I did.

But another thought is creeping up on me, dimming even the beauty of the stars.

God rewards compassion. So does he punish…dis-compassion?

Only now do I realize that my thoughts have been skittering around my sins. Dancing away from them. Trying to avoid deep contemplation of them. But I can't dodge them any longer.

It's not just the girl and the thirteen other people I killed for hard cash. It's every additional person I've used or taken advantage of in my life. I've always given out what was given to me. Whenever I've brushed against compassion, been offered generosity, I've explained it away. But I've reached the end of that. Fr. Jacob's compassion has been genuine. So has Tom's. They'll get nothing from humankind for showing mercy to me. More the opposite. Maybe from God, but not from me or anyone else.

Kindness exists, so maybe love exists too. But I don't know what it feels like.

One of my wishes has been answered. I appreciate life at last. But the second remains…and now I have a new one, a third one, this futile, too-late longing for baptism. The one thing that would have saved me from my sins. From the result of my sins.

From hell.

My throat closes as colder, deathlier terror seeps into my every bone. Pastor Garrett has made sure I know all about hell. Why worry about another few minutes, another half hour, another hour's terror on that gurney? It's what comes afterwards I should be worrying about. And now I've faced up to that, I am.

Is there anything I can do? Since I turned down Fr. Jacob, turned him away, is that it? I'm damned? Taking my eyes from the stars, I stare at my hand, my gun hand, feeling like ravenous beetles are crawling under the skin, like I saw once in a film. Dark, black beetles. My skin remains flat and motionless, though, so I don't try to claw them out. It's just in my mind.

*Fr. Jacob, what do I do? You probably said something, something that would help me. What?*

*Why would God even want to forgive me, anyway?*

Ah. The love-thing again. It all comes down to that.

Actually…Fr. Jacob says God *is* love. Love itself. So is it any wonder that I don't know God, if I don't know love? Or that I don't know love, when I don't know God?

But how do I change that?

A walkie-talkie squawks, and my insides congeal again. I don't hear what's said, but I hear Oatmeal say, "Yes, sir."

His head appears at the window. "Sorry, Jarrold, they're ready now."

I close my eyes and swallow hard. I don't want to go in. I want to stay out here with the stars and these important thoughts that have yet to reach their conclusion. My…my *eternity* may depend on their conclusion.

"You're not going to make us regret letting you stay out there, are you?"

I swallow again. This guy sent my message for me, when he wasn't even supposed to. And I did say I'd go back in. And if I don't, they'll just shoot me. And I'll have no more time at all.

Taking one last look at the sky, I get to my feet, grabbing for the gutter again. It seemed such an easy move, before, but now my legs wobble—I'm going to fall!—but as my feet hit the window ledge, Oatmeal and Ostrich grab me and haul me in. The room still reeks of sick and immediately nausea churns my stomach again. No time for that now. They walk me back out into the passage, barefoot since the slippers are gone. Back towards the execution chamber.

Can God really forgive me? How can it be justice that *I* should be forgiven by *anyone?*

Wait…Fr. Jacob told me something…he told me God judges with justice and mercy, but that He has allowed *us* to choose which one He will judge us with. He quoted something from the Bible, but I can't remember it exactly: "If we judge others with mercy, we will be judged with mercy, but if we judge them only with justice, not mercy, then we will be judged with justice, not with mercy." It was something along those lines. So Fr. Jacob and Tom will be fine, but the judge and Ostrich and the warden and governor and executioner and me—oh yes, *me*, above all, *me*—we've all got some explaining to do, I guess.

But Fr. Jacob said baptism would save me. Take the sin away entirely. But it's too late. Is there nothing else I can do? What did he *say*?

A film I saw as a teenager creeps back into my mind. An assassin has this old priest down on his knees in front of him—reminds me of Fr. Jacob, in hindsight—the priest's being brave, and he asks the assassin, "Are you baptized, son?" I could so see Fr. Jacob acting that way.

Anyway, the assassin's like, "What, you think *my* mother would bother to get me baptized? She hardly bothered to feed me!"

I identified with that assassin so much, back then. My mother certainly never got me baptized. I almost wonder if that film might even have influenced my choices, some years down the line. But the priest…

Oh God, we're at the chamber door already. They're opening it…we're inside.

Sweat breaks out on my forehead again.

Halfway to the gurney, I stop. The blind remains up; the witnesses are still there. Straightening from positions of slumped boredom, their eyes fixed on us. On me. Carl Jarrold, the soulless assassin.

I still can't completely understand how they feel. Because I've never loved anyone or been loved in return. But I do understand now, with sickening, inescapable clarity, how awful it was to kill the people they loved. How wrong.

"Can they hear me?" I'm speaking to Oatmeal, though my eyes don't leave those of the family members. But I don't need a reply; their gazes sharpen, their anger sharpens, like lasers drilling into my soul. They hear me.

The words are so simple, but I can hardly form them. I've never said them before. Never said them and meant them. But I get them out.

"I'm…sorry." It hangs in the air, utterly inadequate. Surely there must be something more to say? But I cannot find words, and no words will make any difference. So I just say it again. "I'm sorry." Then, because it's the only thing I can do that might possibly mean anything to them, I force myself to walk to the gurney and get up onto it. Lie down. I close my eyes and start fighting with my breathing again. With that blasted trembling.

I thought I was scared before but it's nothing to how I feel now. Then I was hoping for heaven and expecting no worse than nothingness.

Now…

*Carl, you are such an idiot, such a* damned *idiot.*

Medical Guy is there the moment Oatmeal and Ostrich finish fastening the restraining straps. He opens the gown, mutters a swearword, actually makes eye contact—to glare at me—and goes to fetch a new set of electrode pads. But he gets them on quicker this time, and soon he's setting to work with his brand new IVs and needles, looking for unpunctured veins. I fight to control my spiraling thoughts, to bring them back to my desperate hunt for answers. Fr. Jacob was right—again. I needed more time for this. Years more time.

That priest in the film... Yes, the assassin's laughing at the priest's question, but the priest just says, "God will forgive you, my son. You only have to ask." And the assassin sticks his gun right in the priest's face and says, "Even for this?" The priest goes a bit paler, but he keeps it together. "Even this," he says. And the assassin shoots him dead. Of course, we thought it hilarious, when we were teenagers. This foolish old priest trying to talk to the tough-as-nails assassin about love and forgiveness when he'd come to kill him!

It doesn't seem remotely funny anymore. The old priest's face has turned into Fr. Jacob's and the imagining is doing something very strange and painful and unfamiliar to my insides that I don't understand.

Oh no, one IV is in place already. Did he manage it quicker this time, or am I just too lost in my head?

I don't have long. I chase the thread of thought again. Yes, that's it...the priest said, "You have only to ask." But what did he mean? Did he mean, "You have only to ask *me* for forgiveness" as in, through baptism? In which case I remain damned. Or did he just have to ask God for the forgiveness? Or did God's forgiveness hinge on the old priest's forgiveness? In which case I'm *so* damned, because my victims are all dead and none of them forgave me before I killed them, and that lot in the viewing gallery were looking pretty taken aback by what I said, but they came to watch me die, they're not going to *forgive* me.

So there's only one possibility that's actually any use to me. That I could just ask God. It seems too easy.

Then again, Fr. Jacob said that all this forgiveness that God gives out, his son Jesus got it for us by dying a very ugly death on a cross. Which isn't exactly what I'd call easy. *I've* got it easy, compared to that, even if the stuff about the anesthesia not working long enough and me suffocating and feeling everything for ten minutes or more is true. God's son had that and more for three *hours*, according to Fr. Jacob.

*Oh God, he's got the second needle in properly. He's taping it in place.*

Fr. Jacob said so much about God's love and forgiveness. And I'm sure there was something about baptism and *desire*. What was it? That…that if you desired baptism enough—but…but couldn't *get* it?—you'd get it anyway? Spiritually…or something? *Was* that it? I just can't remember for certain. Oh, why didn't I pay *attention?* But he *was* always telling me I should speak to God. If there's anything else I can do, I can't see it.

And…I once asked someone what a father was like. He said, well, like another mother. When he realized that was no help to me, he said, well, a parent ought to love you so completely, so unconditionally, that no matter what you do, they will always welcome you home. And Fr. Jacob has always told me God is my father. Tom just said that too. So…

*God? Are you my father? Will you…help me? I don't know what to do. I've totally and utterly messed up everything. My whole life. Probably everyone else's I've come anywhere near. And I'm sorry; I'm so sorry I was so utterly stupid, so blind, so cold, so…so unbelieving.*

*Because…I think you're there. I believe you're there. Even though I've never met you…or felt you. Because…I can imagine what Fr. Jacob would say…he'd say I've gone my whole life without noticing that life is precious and the world is beautiful, so is it any surprise I failed to notice you either? I'm sorry I didn't, I'm so sorry I did all those terrible things, but I don't know what I'm supposed to do! What* can *I do, now? It's too late; I left it too late, just like Fr. Jacob warned me not to! I can't do anything; I'm…I'm about to…to die…*

I am. I really am. Medical Guy has connected the line; he's heading back into One-Way Mirror room. The door clicks shut behind him.

My sins press around me like black mud, sucking me down, crushing, drowning me. I can feel tears sliding down my cheeks but I can't stop them. Any moment now…

*God…God…I wish I could love you. I wish I could love you the way Fr. Jacob loves you. But I don't know how. I wish I could feel your love, then maybe I would know how to do it. This love thing… I'm sorry… I deserve to go to hell, I do. It's pathetic of me to be begging for mercy…after what I've done. If you send me to hell, I'll understand. But…please don't…please…please forgive me, the way Fr. Jacob always said you—*

I feel it. The cold liquid entering my veins. Through my right arm. The line is working. It's over. According to the proponents, I have thirty seconds left. Thirty seconds before I'm unconscious. According to the opponents, I have up to five minutes and then I may wake up again too soon. Okay, that last sentence didn't make sense, but I know what I mean.

I clamp my teeth together to keep from panting in terror, but in my mind I'm screaming.

*God, please, please, please, forgive me, forgive me, PLEASE…*

My head swims…a heavy sensation is settling over my body.

*Please, please, please…*

A door bangs open. Raised voices—one of them very familiar: "I'm eighty next month, don't crush my arm—I'm his spiritual advisor, so get out of my way."

"But spiritual advisors have to sit in the *gallery*—"

I struggle to open my eyes, but lead weights hold them closed.

"You can't be in here, Father!" Oatmeal…

"Are you a good Catholic, Tomas Flores? Then *get your hands off me.*"

"*Father!*" Tom sounds anguished.

But he must have let go, because the next moment a hand grips mine and someone is leaning close to me, a familiar scent of incense tickling my nose. "Carl, it's Father Jacob, can you hear me?"

"Yes…" I try to nod as well, but I'm not sure I succeed. My whole body feels leaden.

Fr. Jacob's fumbling with something… Ostrich's voice cuts in… "You can't give him water!" Tom responds, "It's Holy Water, you idiot, it's not for drinking…" but Fr. Jacob leans close again, speaking very fast and clear, "Carl, do you renounce Satan and believe in God the Father, Jesus his Son, and the Holy Spirit?"

My tongue feels heavy too; my mind filling with fog. "*Yes…*"

Water splashes onto my forehead, running into my closed eyes, once, twice, three times. "Carl, I baptize you in the name of the Father, and of the Son, and of the Holy Spirit…" A finger traces a cross in the water. This is it…the sacrament… *baptism.*

And wonderfully, irrationally, the fear eases its grip.

I try to smile, to tell Fr. Jacob I know what he's done for me. I think I manage it, just.

The warden's voice booms through the speakers: "This is an execution chamber, not a church! *Get him* out of here *right now!*"

The gurney jolts under me…someone is trying to pull Fr. Jacob away and he must be holding on. Medicine and age— his breath stirs my hair as he leans very close to my ear, gripping my hand tightly again. "Carl, you are an adopted child of God and your sins are forgiven. Go to our Father in peace; I'll see you soon." His lips brush my forehead, then his hand is yanked from mine; I can hear him being dragged away: "All right, put me down, I can walk, I can walk…"

My head swims…Fr. Jacob's gone…and I'm *forgiven*. I abandon my struggle for consciousness. Darkness creeps up and swallows me…

I'm standing on a hill with fourteen people crowding around me. I don't have to count them. I know there are fourteen of them but still I flinch when I actually *look* at them. It's them, it's my victims, the people I killed. I open my mouth to say…what? Sorry? But they rush in on me, grab me and drag me to where a huge wooden cross is laid out on the ground.

"Justice," they hiss, "Justice! Justice!" The banker lifts a heavy hammer, the girl rushes forward with a bucket full of five-inch metal spikes; the others push me down on the cross, spread out my arms… God, they're going to *nail me* to this thing!

"Wait…" I whisper. "*Wait*, please, I'm *sorry*…"

"Let's not do this," says a voice. "He is our brother, after all." It's the activist, the one the corporation paid me to kill. The one I've always been most sure I'll meet in heaven. The one whose parents sent me that strange letter, saying they forgave me.

But they turn on him like a pack of angry animals; I'm pulled up and pushed away, and they're spreading him out on that cross instead, readying the nails. I watch, appalled. *I'm* the one who did something wrong. "Wait…" My voice wavers weakly. I don't want to go back on there. But… "Wait, you mustn't—"

But they're driving the nails in, and suddenly it's not the activist on there, it's Fr. Jacob, his face twisted in pain. "No!"

46

I rush forward but hands grab me, hold me back. "NO! Don't! It was me! It wasn't him, it was *me!* Stop! *It was me!* Let him go!"

I'm screaming at the top of my voice, struggling, but they just finish nailing poor Fr. Jacob to the thing and haul it upright. His frail body jerks, contorts in agony as he struggles to breathe.

"No! I'm sorry! I'm sorry! I'm so sorry…!" I'm sobbing, but I still can't get free, can't help him, can't take his place…

But Fr. Jacob looks down at me and smiles through the pain. Except it's not quite Fr. Jacob anymore. He looks more like the man from the cross in the prison chapel. Jesus. But the way he smiles at me is the way Fr. Jacob sometimes smiles at me. The way that makes me feel better about myself and everything, though I'm not sure why.

"I'm sorry," I whisper, but he just smiles even more tenderly. And somehow I know that he is happy to be up there instead of me, that it's okay. I can't struggle any more. I collapse to my knees and now I'm whispering, "*Thank you…thank you…thank you so much…*"

The scene swirls and dissolves…I'm back in the blackness of my head. My eyes won't open. I'm dimly aware I'm lying flat on my back, something cold running into my arm. Did I pass right out? Fr. Jacob…he *was* here. Wasn't he? He baptized me…I'm forgiven…yes, my forehead is wet— no hallucination, that. He barged in and baptized me. *Thank you, Fr. Jacob, thank you, God.*

But the relief…finding myself here…it's huge—such a vivid dream. But it's okay, Fr. Jacob's not being crucified…or maybe he is…watching me die. But perhaps, now, it's not quite so bad.

*Lord…please don't let him leave it too late.* Fr. Jacob's desperate prayer yesterday whispers through my mind and despite the soul-soothing calm my baptism has wrapped me in, a shiver of horror goes through me at the realization—it *should have been* too late for me. If everything had gone right, as it usually does…I'd have got no further than wondering why I was scared: and then I'd have been dead.

Dead and damned. Like how many others?

Another icy not-physical shudder runs through me. *Oh, thank God the execution was botched, thank God.* Never thought I'd say *that*.

Fr. Jacob's prayer whispers through my mind again. Did God mess up the first set of lines because He likes Fr. Jacob so much? The thought makes me want to…*giggle*—God wrecking the State's timetable for the old priest's sake—but I can't speak, I can't move, my body feels so heavy…more cool liquid runs into my arm…is it wash, have I had the second drug, the paralytic, already? I'm by no means unconscious enough for my liking…I'm far from entirely with it but I sure as anything am not unconscious.

Never mind. What does it matter? I'm forgiven. This is nothing. Nothing compared to what my forgiveness cost. I can see that man again, there on that hill…there in *my* place…

My chest aches, my lungs screaming as the drug prevents my muscles working. But I surely appear to be unconscious.

Fr. Jacob won't know how much it hurts. That's good. *God, it hurts.*

I accept the pain. I try to embrace it. I deserve it. I deserve so much more, but this is all I will have to pay. What a wonder that is.

I'm suffocating…suffocating without even being able to gasp for air, my diaphragm stilled by the drug…and another wave of coldness rushes into my arm…wash? No, it's the heart-stopper…because it's burning, burning wherever it touches, burning like acid, coals, hot pokers, fire in my veins…but that's easy to ignore, because one final realization spirals into my mind…

Fr. Jacob's gentle kiss, his words of kindness… That was *love.* Love shown to *me*… Because what could he gain from me? He had me signed up, another member of the God-club. There was absolutely nothing more he could possibly get. But still, he offered me that comfort…for free…because he loves the lost sheep he brought home…

I've felt love.

That's what I've *been* feeling, when he looks at me that way, the way Jesus smiled at me…

It's how *God* loves me. The understanding surges through me, pushing aside the burning pain and the agonizing need for air that's starting to gray out my fuddled mind. That is how God loves me.

Unconditionally.

And I understand, now, why watching Fr. Jacob suffer hurt so much… Because I care about him. I love him. There is no further use I can possibly make of him, yet *I still care*. It's *love*. He's taught me how to love.

And how to accept love…

And finally, oh, finally, I can feel Him there. Like a father holding out His arms. A father Who's been holding them out for a long, long time.

I am loved. I always was. The extra time wasn't for Fr. Jacob's sake. It was for *Carl*…

Joy sweeps through me.

Blackness follows, blackness that devours everything in its path…

But I simply allow myself to fall into that loving embrace—and for the first time in my life I am truly happy and completely at peace.

**We cannot love unless we are first loved.**

*St Augustine, Sermon 34*

---

### *You can make a difference!*

Reviews and recommendations are vital to any author's success. If you liked this book, please write a short review—a few lines are enough—and tell your friends about the book too.

You will help the author to create new stories and allow others to share your enjoyment.

*Your support is important. Thank you.*

# DON'T MISS

# A CHANGING OF THE GUARD

## A Sequel to THREE LAST THINGS

### A DYING PRIEST. A BOTCHED EXECUTION.
### A YOUNG MAN ON THE BRINK.

Tomas Flores hates serving on the prison's Death Squad—and now he may be about to lose his job thanks to his actions during Carl Jarrold's hellish execution. Desperate and conflicted, where can he turn?

Father Jacob Thompson has spent decades opening his heart to convicted murderers—only to watch them die. Now his last black sheep is safely gathered in and he's ready to rest—but will the Lord let him?

If you loved the tense, "psychologically-compelling," spiritual thriller Three Last Things: or, the Hounding of Carl Jarrold, Soulless Assassin, then this heart-wrenching, emotionally-taut sequel is for you.

# TURN OVER FOR
# A SNEAK PEEK!

# A CHANGING OF THE GUARD Sneak Peak

The execution doesn't take as long as usual. Well, how can it? From Carl's rapidly fading consciousness as I baptized him, the first drug was already in his veins. I've missed all the lead-in.

How *much* lead-in? What caused this extraordinary delay? It should've been over about an hour ago. No matter. Chest tight with an all-too-familiar anguish that has nothing to do with the physical pain gnawing my body, I push the questions from my mind. Keeping my eyes on Carl's unconscious— *please, Lord?*—body there on the death gurney, I resist the urge to close my eyes. Always feels too much like abandonment.

Apparently, I'm more interesting than Carl—at any rate, I feel the gaze of the viewing gallery's other occupants on me. I vaguely recall glimpsing only four people as Tom and his comrade marched me in and deposited me in this chair, so I am clearly in with the press/official witness/family of the convicted—not that there will be any of the latter present. Unlikely they would dump me in with the victims' relatives, after the show I just put on in the execution chamber.

If I so much as make eye contact, the press will be on me. I concentrate on Carl, on praying for Carl, although judging by his peaceful smile at the end, after I had washed his grievous sins away, he is heading straight into his heavenly Father's arms. I suspect it would have been an open and shut case of baptism by desire if I hadn't made it in time, but it's nice to be certain. *Carl* definitely needed that certainty.

In fact...yes, he has arrived. After what felt like twenty minutes, so was probably only ten, they are pronouncing him dead. A glimpse of young Tomas Flores' tense face as he steps forward and hits the button to lower the blinds over the observation windows is enough to confirm the monumental foul-up I already suspect, though I am none the wiser as to how exactly it unfolded.

Well, however bad it was, Carl is well out of it now. Unlike me.

The gazes of the press and official witnesses press on me even harder, so, emotionally as well as physically exhausted, I opt for bowing my head, closing my eyes and praying some more as a couple of tears make cool tracks down my cheeks. After the way I had to struggle past two prison guards to reach Carl in the execution chamber, I am still far too tired to do anything but sit quietly. Indeed, I'm not sure I will summon the energy to stand ever again. I must have been running on pure adrenaline. How else does a half-dead almost-eighty-year-old prevail over two healthy young men? Well, the spiritual and emotional blackmail sure did help.

The door to the observation room clicks open, and a moment later I sense someone stop in front of me.

"Father Jacob?"

I open my eyes—stiffly raise my head. "Hello, Tom." Still pinch-eyed and anxious. Perhaps I should call him Officer Flores. I don't know him well. But he doesn't seem to notice.

"The relatives are...are asking for you."

Of course they are. I should have seen that coming. "Right. Just give me a moment." I pull a bottle of water and two types of pills from my bag. Heavy-duty painkillers and some even more vicious stimulants I talked out of my sympathetic doctor. It is too soon to have more of either, but I take two of each, anyway, fumbling and almost dropping them. My hands shake all the time these days. Bag repacked, I attempt to crank my head back far enough to look up at Tom. "Okay. Lend me your strong, young arm, then."

He reaches out and takes my spindly limb as though he is afraid it might come off in his hand, just the way he did earlier. The bruises are going to be on the other side, where his partner grabbed me. His non-Catholic partner, I would guess.

I set the end of my stick to the floor and attempt to push myself up. Tom provides a bit more assistance when it becomes clear how necessary it is and somehow I am standing. As I shuffle towards the door, leaning equally on Prison Officer Flores and my trusty stick, one of the reporters finally manages to make eye contact with me.

"And how do you feel about all this, Father Jacob?" he chirps brightly.

I'm wearing my prison chaplain badge and they have had ample chance to read it. No doubt I will feature in their lurid accounts of whatever went on here today.

I hold tight to my supporting arm and keep shuffling, consumed with a passionate desire to reach the door. "How anyone who has just watched their friend killed in front of them feels, I imagine."

Tom flinches. Hmm. I wasn't getting at him but he is clearly feeling bad. And it is not like he is some fresh new guard. Just what did happen?

"Did you consider Carl Jarrold a friend, Father Jacob?"

"Yes."

"Despite the fact he was a hired killer?"

"Yes."

"Do you condone his actions?"

"No." I'm too tired for lengthy replies, especially to stupid questions.

"What are you going to say to his victims' relatives?"

Tom eases me through the door before I have to reply. I used to be good at this stuff, but I am just so tired. The press are one thing too many, and I am saving my stolen energy for the relatives.

A short way along the passage I pause and look up at Tom. I swear, even a year ago the kid wasn't that tall. He is well past gaining extra inches, so it's me shrinking...if I could only *straighten* properly... "So what happened? Don't let me go in there blind."

Tom's Adam's apple bobs as he swallows. "It...both IV lines failed. *Both* of them. Eventually they had to let us take Car...the prisoner to the john while they set up completely new equipment. It worked the second time. Well, you saw. It was..." His voice cracks slightly. "It was awful."

Awful. Yes. I imagine the scene and wince. "How did...Carl take it?"

"Seemed calm to start with, but by the time it started to go wrong he was scared. Really scared. Tried not to show it but..." He draws in a sharp breath. "An hour. That's how long they had him on there. It—" He breaks off again, shaking his head, misery in his youthful brown eyes.

My heart aches for him—and Carl. The unexpected delay probably saved my friend's soul, but I still feel for what he went through.

I shuffle on down the corridor, and Tom paces beside me as though in slow-motion until we reach the relatives' debriefing room.

*Lord, may your love be in my heart and on my lips. Let me be nothing but your mouthpiece here.*

As I make my slow entrance, ten or fifteen pairs of eyes pin me like a butterfly to a card. I straighten up with effort, lifting my heavy head as I seek to get a proper look at them. Today will probably be the only time I ever meet them in person, but names, faces, and horrible, tragic stories fill my head. I read all the news reports, watched all the footage, wanting to know them, so that my knowing might help make them real people to Carl—not that it really worked with him.

I let go of Tom at last—the adrenaline is back and the drugs are kicking in—and move to the closest woman, reaching out with my wrinkled hand to stiffly enclose hers. "Mrs. Rafaela, I'm so sorry for your loss. I've heard so many good things about your son."

She says nothing, simply watches me, brows drawn slightly together, as I turn to the next person. "Mr. Hyson, I'm so sorry for your loss..."

I manage to greet four of them before a red-faced man pushes to the front and speaks roughly.

"What's all this 'I'm sorry for your loss' nonsense? I thought Carl Jarrold was your buddy, you pathetic crow?"

Some of them look away, unwilling to be associated with this, but others square their jaws and glare at me.

"I counted Carl as a friend," I say quietly, "and I am overjoyed that he turned to God in the nick of time, but what he did to your loved ones was inexcusable and every single day since I met him I have prayed for you all and for him."

The red-faced man lurches forward, his fist clenched. "Don't you dare put us in the same sentence as that monster."

Tom frowns, moving forward slightly, but I wave him back. I don't need protecting. Especially not today.

"I have prayed for you all in the same sentence for three years, and I am not about to stop now."

His fist clenches again, wavers, re-clenches. My refusal to

back down confuses him. I can almost *see* the pain and hate eating him from inside and I wish I had words that would help, but I doubt he will listen to me, not today. Not after...

I look around at them all, searching their faces. Though we will only ever be together this once, so fleetingly, still I feel like I've known them for years—like in some strange way, they too are part of my flock. "Are you all right?" I ask. "You must have mixed feelings about what you just witnessed."

The official counselor, waiting in the corner, shoots me an irate look. I stole her opening line.

The red-faced man—Philip Masson's father, Hugh, his name is—snorts. "Mixed? Hardly. I've got a bottle of champagne waiting at home."

But few of the eyes looking back at me are as blasé as his.

"I knew..." The woman—Tina Beattrie?—breaks off. Frowns. Finally speaks again. "I knew...this...wouldn't bring my Rob back. But...when it was over if felt like...it felt like I only just realized that it...that it wouldn't bring him back. That probably sounds crazy."

"I felt exactly that way." Another woman whispers it. Gina Toombs? They catch each other's eyes and fall into a tight embrace.

"I'm glad it went so badly wrong." A middle-aged woman speaks flatly, her face hard. Sheila, isn't it? "He got what he deserved."

Tom folds his arms, his head hunching slightly, brows bunching as though he is trying not to glower. Something about what she just said did not go down well with him.

The man standing beside the woman nods, his whole body tense. "If it'd gone right...what sort of punishment would that be, so nice and peaceful?"

A couple of a similar age, standing with their arms around each other's waists, shake their heads. "No, it was barbaric," says the woman. "I just felt so sorry for him. When they brought him back in—the look on his face. I'd have given anything to call it off."

The man nods and a few people murmur agreement.

"You bunch of bleeding hearts," retorts Hugh Masson. "It was justice!"

"Maybe it was," says an older gentleman. Who...? Ah, Paul Grignon's grandfather. "But I do wonder now how I ever thought this would make me feel better." He speaks calmly, unmoved—unashamed—at sharing. "I just thought that I'd be able to let it all go after this. But now...I've got this burned into my brain instead. If they'd just locked him up and thrown away the key three years ago it would all have been over and done with."

Hugh Masson and Sheila both open their mouths, scowling at the older man, but the counselor, looking alarmed, steps forward and starts shepherding people into chairs to begin the official debrief and counseling session. She glances pointedly from me to the door. No one has actually asked me straight out why I burst in and baptized Carl Jarrold, the evil assassin, but I guess they could tell I meant it when I called Carl my friend, and whether I genuinely loved him was what they really wanted to know.

I smile and shake as many hands as I can. "It was so lovely to meet you at last. Wish it could have been under different circumstances. I will be praying for you. Please pray for me."

Philip Masson and Sheila and her partner recoil from my hand as from a poisonous snake, but everyone else accepts my goodbyes and good wishes, albeit with a variety of expressions on their faces. Silently, I bless the group, then I take Tom's arm again to shuffle out, the thin fabric of my cassock feeling like a heavy tarpaulin pressing against my legs, impeding my progress.

Tom's radio bleeps as we get outside. He raises it briefly to his ear—"Yes, sir"—then hooks it back at his belt. "Uh." He swallows, Adam's apple bobbing. "Warden wants to see you, *Padre.*"

I bet he does. "Well, I'm going back to Carl first. Only the relatives take priority over that. The warden can wait."

I try to shuffle onwards, but Tom holds tight to my arm, not moving.

"*Padre?*" Anxiety almost overflows from him, now.

"Yes?"

"How did... How did you know Jarrold wanted to be baptized? The warden...he's going to ask. What are you going to tell him?"

I stare up into his guilty eyes. I cannot believe this good-hearted young man snuck a phone on shift with him, but he is the one Carl's message came via, isn't he? He got it out to me, somehow, as I waited in the prison chapel, praying and wondering why no one came to tell me it was over, still watching my phone with hopeless hope. And the consequences of that message—me barging into the execution chamber—are serious enough that he's worried how much trouble he is going to be in.

"The Holy Spirit let me know."

"That's...what you're actually going to tell him?"

"That is what I will tell him."

"He's not going to accept that."

"What else can he do? Beat it out of me?"

59

Tom looks me over, his gaze hovering between pity and concern—then his lip quirks, finally, into a slight smile. "Nah, I doubt that."

"So do I. So he will have to accept it. It's the truth, anyway. The Holy Spirit did let me know." I pat Tom's hand where it rests on my arm, managing not to wallop him with my stick, and we move on.

The corridor has been extended while we were in the debrief room, a good hundred miles added to its length. Only the need to return to Carl drives me on. I would never normally leave an executed person's side until the funeral directors arrive to take charge of their mortal remains. Not that I think Carl minds. He is probably in the middle of an emotional reunion with some of the relatives' loved ones right now.

Finally, finally, we reach the door of the execution chamber. Tom makes no attempt to stop my entry this time—in fact, he opens the door for me. My gaze runs over Carl, the gurney, the bleak room. The bleak, *empty* room.

"Is there any chance of a chair?"

"Of course. I'll bring one in."

I release his arm, freeing him to depart on his errand of mercy, and trudge—shuffle—determinedly across the vast three meter distance to where Carl lies. Gripping the edge of the gurney—better support than my stick—I look down at the body of the young man lying there. Healthy; toned muscles; only a few years older than Tom, the sheer waste of it hits me harder than ever. How does this make up for the tragic theft of his victims' lives? Waste piled upon waste— maybe, finally, belatedly, Carl is outraged by this too. Outraged with himself, at least.

*What a mess you made of your life, Carl.* I rest an aching,

60

shaking hand on his dark hair, still damp with sweat and holy water. *Oh, thank you, Lord, that he found you in time.*

"Yes, I think you redefined *leaving it until the last moment* today, you know," I murmur, not sure if I am speaking to Carl or the Almighty.

I move my hand to the buckles holding Carl's right arm down and stiffly work the first one undone. Then the second. I fold his arm across his chest, wishing it a little less muscley and *heavy*, then inch my way around the gurney to free the other one. Crossing that one over the other makes me pant, dots dancing in my vision. I am almost done.

In every possible way.

I bend, placing a kiss on Carl's forehead just as I did earlier. It's cool, now, his face slack and empty, but I know where he is. Or rather, Who he is with.

That precious knowledge finally breaks through the familiar post-execution numbness, hitting me like a sledgehammer, doubling me over that gurney, my forehead pressing to the cold metal, the top of my head pushing against Carl as I gasp for breath. But the ragged sobs that tear from my throat are pure relief, pure joy.

*Thank you, Lord. Thank you. Thank you.*

Never have I been so afraid that a precious soul entrusted to my care would be lost. This last year, as my body failed around me and I could do less and less, I prioritized Carl. Even when forced to let go of everything else, I refused to give up on him.

Now...now, thanks to the Holy Spirit, he is safe. *Thank you, Lord. Thank you.*

Young Tom will be back soon enough hauling one of those heavy metal padded chairs from the gallery—I should try and recover my dignity. But I'm not sure I have the energy.

Carl is safe. Carl is with the Lord. Since the chances of me being able to stand up long enough to celebrate his funeral...well, requiem Mass, now...weren't looking too good, I've already made all the necessary arrangements. He doesn't need me anymore.

Yes...Carl doesn't need me anymore.

The realization lifts an immense weight from my shoulders, a crushing spiritual tonnage that's been growing, growing, growing over the last three years.

Apparently it is the only thing that has been keeping me upright, because the utter exhaustion that sweeps me is like nothing I have experienced before.

My legs buckle—my bodyweight instantly overcomes my feeble grasp on the gurney and the floor rushes up to meet me. Pain flares through my hip and side, a moment before my head also smacks against the hard linoleum—and doesn't fade, despite the cocktail of drugs in my system.

My breathing—or maybe my heart, I can hardly tell— stutters oddly. I have an inhaler in my bag but I doubt I can reach it and I don't care to try. It feels like I have been putting Him off for weeks—months—but finally I am free to go to Him.

*Carl doesn't need me anymore.* My lips try to smile, then abandon the effort. Shadows blur my vision. I close my eyes and lie quietly, waiting, pain too familiar these days to trouble me.

*Lord, I am so ready for You. I hope You are ready for me.*

Peace fills me, cradles me. There is nothing more for me to worry about. No one who needs anything from me. No needy soul with a claim on my heart...

*Clatter-clang-thud.* Footsteps rush towards me.

62

A frantic voice. "Father Jacob? Father Jacob! *Oh God...*"

Bleeping, buzzing, beeping... The words fade in and out. "...Father Jacob...execution chamber...call an ambulance..."

Hands grip my shoulders, shake me. Pain spikes from my hip, making me gasp. The shaking stops abruptly, but the volume increases.

*"Father Jacob?* Father Jacob? *¡Por favor! Talk to me!"*

His voice echoes strangely in my ears. I drag my eyes open again. A young, anxious face blurs in and out of focus. Troubled. For some reason, another face flashes through my mind—that young guard in Tennesee who shot himself in the prison parking lot after an execution a few years back.

I still can't breathe...

Hands fumble at my wrist, checking the medical bracelet there. More rummaging beside me—my inhaler touches my lips. Those beseeching eyes...so much pain and potential...I take it.

It doesn't help much. The ceiling swims, his voice echoes more and more. I cannot make out what he is saying. Cannot see him. But his desperation latches onto my soul.

*Ah, fine, one more. Just one more. Yes, I want to help him, Lord. But I will need another day. So it is entirely up to you.*

*Always is...*

*Your will...*

Soft blackness enfolds me.

And swallows me whole.

# The Boy Who Knew

## FRIENDS IN HIGH PLACES: CARLO ACUTIS

## DEAD? DEFINE DEAD.

*"You have leukemia."*

Daniel's just received the worst news a teen can get. The adults in his life are crumbling under the shock. In desperation, he turns to his parish priest for help and is introduced to a boy his age, Carlo Acutis—who just happens to be dead.

Daniel's convinced the priest is wasting his time. But as he struggles to come to terms with his uncertain future an unlikely friendship develops between him and the holy dead boy—who may not be quite so dead after all.

*The Boy Who Knew* is the first title in Carnegie Medal nominee Corinna Turner's new 'Friends in High Places' series. If you've always been interested in the saints but find dry biographies boring and hard to get through, this fast-paced story is for you.

*"Powerful and inspiring."*
**SUSAN PEEK**, author of the
God's Forgotten Friends series

*"beautifully honest"*
**KARINA FABIAN**,
author of *Discovery*

## AVAILABLE AS A PAPERBACK AND EBOOK
## IN ENGLISH, ITALIAN & SPANISH

## THE BOY WHO KNEW (CARLO ACUTIS) Sneak Peek

*"You have leukemia."*

I keep seeing the doctor's eyes over his mask, darting from me to my parents. I keep hearing his words in my head. Mum burst into tears. Dad started pounding on the doctor's desk with his fists. Me, I just sat there.

Leukemia. How can I have leukemia? I'm fifteen. Stuff that bad doesn't happen to people my age, right?

But the tiredness... The bruising...

*"You have leukemia."*

When we got home from the hospital, Mum started getting ready for the Vigil Mass as usual. Dad never comes along, these days, but tonight...tonight he started yelling at Mum *how could she possibly think there was a God if He could let this happen to me? How could she think He was good?* And Mum shouted back that *God was my only hope, couldn't he see that? Did he want me to die?*

They were still screaming at each other when I slipped out of the house and walked to church. I don't think I've ever come to church on my own before. I felt really self-conscious. Any other week I'd have grabbed the chance to skip Mass. Today, I am angry with God, I suppose? But I'm also really, really scared. And I just wanted to escape the shouting.

Mum never showed up for Mass. I got a text during the first reading: *Daniel, where are you?* I texted back: *At church.* An old lady glared at me over the top of her un-environmentally friendly single-use mask.

Then I fell asleep during the homily. I'm just so tired all the time. I got glared at again.

Now everyone's gone, and I'm still sitting here. I'm afraid to go home in case they're still arguing. Or in case they want to talk about it all. I feel numb. I haven't even taken my mask off, though I'm alone.

*"You have leukemia."*

*"Do you want Daniel to die?"*

Am I going to die? Words from one of the readings I heard before I nodded off come into my mind: *There is no need to worry; but if there is anything you need, pray for it.*

"God, please don't let me die," I whisper.

God doesn't reply. Maybe Dad's right. Pulling my mask of at last, I shove it into my pocket, hands shaking.

"God, I'm scared."

Nothing. Well, except that the numbness shatters and, suddenly, I really *feel* the fear, turning my belly into a black hole, cold as a...a...a morgue?

I bury my face in my hands as the sobs rip from me. *Am I going to die, Lord?*

Distant footsteps from the front of the church.

They pause, then tread briskly along the aisle. Towards me. Oh no.

I wipe my face, desperately trying to stop the gasping, heaving sobs. Snot smears my sleeve. Yuck.

"Hi, Daniel."

Reluctantly, I glance up, my shoulders still shuddering. It's Father Thomas. He's young and kinda cool, sweeping around in his long black dress—sorry, *cassock*—without a trace of embarrassment. I wish I had his total lack of self-consciousness.

"Hi, Father." My voice wobbles. *Play it cool, Daniel. Just pretend you're fine and get up and leave.*

"Are you okay?"

"No." I'm shaking my head. What happened to leaving? And then I'm blurting, "I've got leukemia."

His lips part as though I just punched him in the gut. "Oh, Daniel…" He settles into the next wide-spaced pew, sitting sideways to face me, eyes narrowed in concern. "Heck, I thought you were going to say bullying or something. That's a hard thing to face, at your age. When are you starting treatment? Did they say…what the prognosis is?"

"Prognosis?" I sound like an idiot. Oh, whether I'm going to live or die, he means. "Oh, uh…well, I just got the preliminary test result today. After more tests on Monday morning, the specialists make a plan and I see them the next Monday and…well, that's when they'll tell me…y'know. They think I'll start treatment almost at once."

"That's good. Just time for a novena, too."

"What?"

He pulls out his wallet and flicks through several business cards before pulling one out. "This is the saint for you. Well, a Blessed, technically. In fact, he's not a Blessed until next Saturday, so I shouldn't really be giving these new cards out yet, but under the circumstances. Here. Almost-Blessed Carlo Acutis. He had leukemia when he was fifteen. Best prayer buddy you could have right now. I think there's a novena on his website."

He sees my vague look. "A novena's when you team up with a saint for nine days to pray for something."

"Oh yeah, I remember." I accept the card and slip it into my pocket, though I'm not sure I want it. Now the numbness has gone, I am starting to feel pretty mad at God. Isn't He supposed to love me? A wire of white-hot rage tightens painfully around my insides, and I scowl towards the tabernacle. Dad's right, how could He let this happen to me? What did I ever do to Him?

"Have you ever made a pot?" asks Father Thomas, suddenly. "Or a painting?"

What? "Uh, I make 3D art on my computer. Loads of it."

"Ah, that's right. I knew you were an artist of some kind. Say if you created a 3D pot, then. Did anyone force you to make it?"

I look at him blankly. "No. I just do it because I want to."

"Could you, like, virtually smash it?"

"In my program? Sure. More or less." A surge of happiness flows through me at the thought of my state-of-the-art 3D design program and extensive inventory of quality assets...then wilts. What good will it all do me if I can't beat this thing?

"Could you take the pieces of your ex-pot and make them into a mosaic that was far, far more beautiful?"

"If I wanted to."

"And that would be okay? Breaking your pot and

68

remaking it into something better?"

"Of course. It's my pot. I made it, right?"

"And then you could keep your beautiful mosaic forever, right?"

Forever? I may not have a *year*, for all I know... Belatedly, I figure out what he's on about. "Oh, very clever! I'm not a *pot!* It's not the same!"

"No, it's not the same," Father Thomas agrees, unperturbed. "We're far, far more important to God than some 3D pot. Or even a real one. He loves every single hair on our heads—and he knows exactly how many there are."

"Great!" I snap, leaping up from the pew and storming away from his infuriating calm. I yell over my shoulder, "I'll be sure to remember that when they start falling out!"

But I catch his soft words, just before I slip through the door.

"I hope you do."

**Get THE BOY WHO KNEW (CARLO ACUTIS) from your favorite retailer today!**

# ACKNOWLEDGMENTS

I'd like to thank Carolyn Astfalk, Penny and Andy C., Fr. Paul C., Regina Doman, Elizabeth Amy Hajek, Katy Huth Jones, Susan Peek, Andrea Jo Rodgers, Victoria Seed, and Theo T. for all their excellent editorial help.

Special thanks go to Victoria Seed, Profanity Consultant Extraordinaire.

Thanks to my parents for all their support, and to my Mum for her honest critiques.

And not forgetting St. Maximilian Kolbe, the patron of this book, and last but the opposite of least, the Holy Spirit, who hounded me so mercilessly into writing it.

---

# ABOUT THE AUTHOR

Corinna Turner has been writing since she was fourteen and likes strong protagonists with plenty of integrity. She has an MA in English from Oxford University, but has foolishly gone on to work with both children and animals! Juggling work with the disabled and being a midwife to sheep, she spends as much time as she can in a little hut at the bottom of the garden, writing.

She is a Catholic Christian with roots in the Methodist and Anglican churches. A keen cinema-goer, she lives in the UK. She used to have a Giant Snail called Peter with a 6½" long shell, but now makes do with a cactus and a campervan!

**Sign up** for **free short stories** & **news** at:
*www.UnSeenBooks.com*

**Get in touch with Corinna:**
Facebook: Corinna Turner - Twitter: @CorinnaTAuthor

Made in United States
Cleveland, OH
21 May 2025

17093624R00049